This fun **Phonics** reader

belongs to

_____

Ladybird Reading
Phonics
BOOK 12

Contents

A catalogue record for this book is available from the British Library

Published by Ladybird Books Ltd
80 Strand London WC2R 0RL
A Penguin Company

2 4 6 8 10 9 7 5 3 1
© LADYBIRD BOOKS LTD MMVI
LADYBIRD and the device of a Ladybird are trademarks of Ladybird Books Ltd

ISBN-13: 978-1-84646-321-1
ISBN-10: 1-84646-321-1

Printed in Italy

Bella's Bedspread

by Clive Gifford
illustrated by Stephen Holmes

introducing the ea spelling of the
short **e** sound, as in head and bread

Bella had a secret treasure.
It was a magic feather
bedspread, and it could fly!

Whatever the weather,
Bella's bedspread flew
steadily.

This is heavenly!

Heather Deadwood lived next door to Bella. She was dreadfully jealous of Bella's magic bedspread.

One morning, as Bella got
her breakfast ready, Heather
crept into Bella's house.

Heather leapt onto Bella's bed. "Ready bedspread, steady bedspread, GO!" she said.

Heather wanted to have a pleasant ride, but instead…

10

Ooo, my head...

Heather was
soon breathless
and dizzy.

Which just goes to show that jealousy can be very bad for your health.

Mr Reardon-Beardon's
Beard

by Mandy Ross
illustrated by Carla Daly

introducing the **ear** sound,
as in clear and beard

"Beards are in fashion this year."

"So I hear, my dear,"
said Mr Reardon-Beardon.

So Mr Reardon-Beardon
bought some beard-grower.

He smeared the cream on his
face from
ear to ear.

His beard grew…

and grew…

and grew…

until it reached
from here...

to here.

"It's too long, my dear,"
said Mrs Reardon-Beardon, and
she put the beard around
his ears.

"Now I've got an ear-wig,"
said Mr Reardon-Beardon.

"An earwig in your beard?
Oh dear!" cried
Mrs Reardon-Beardon.

"Not an earwig, my dear," said Mr Reardon-Beardon more clearly. "A wig for my ears!"

Christine's Knitted Knickers

by Mandy Ross
illustrated by Angie Sage

introducing silent letters

Christine found some balls
of lambswool. They were khaki,
white and red.

"If I knew how to knit, I could knit some knickers," she said.

So she and a friend went to
Knitting School, to find out
what to do.

Geoff soon knitted a woolly
scarf in stitches of red and blue.

"Crumbs – I'm all thumbs and my knitting's in a knot," said Christine, getting cross.

Though she soon learned just
how to knit with help
from Mrs Moss.

The finished knickers were rather wrinkled, and the stitches itched a lot.

Don't laugh, Geoff...

But they were great for keeping Christine's teapot nice and hot.

HOW TO USE
Phonics
BOOK 12

The fun stories in this book introduce your child to words including the ear sound, the 'ea' spelling of the short e sound (as in 'bread'), and silent letters. They will help your child begin reading words including these sounds and spellings.

- Read each story through to your child first. Familiarity helps children to identify some of the words and phrases.

- Have fun talking about the sounds and pictures together – what repeated sound can your child hear in Bella's Bedspread? And in Mr Reardon-Beardon's Beard?

- Help your child break new words into separate sounds (eg. h-ea-d) and blend their sounds together to say the word.

- Point out how words with the same written ending sound the same. If y-ear says 'year', what does cl-ear say?

- Some common words, such as 'could', 'some' and even 'the', can't be read by sounding out. Help your child practise recognising words like these.

Phonic fun

Christine's knitted knickers

This story introduces your child to the idea of silent letters, such as the 'h' in 'white' or the 'w' in 'whole'. Help your child get to grips with common silent letter spellings and try to think of other examples of words with silent letters in.

Ladybird Reading

Phonics

Phonics is part of the Ladybird Reading range. It can be used alongside any other reading programme, and is an ideal way to practise the reading work that your child is doing, or about to do in school.

Ladybird has been a leading publisher of reading programmes for the last fifty years. **Phonics** combines this experience with the latest research to provide a rapid route to reading success.

The fresh quirky stories in Ladybird's twelve **Phonics** storybooks are designed to help your child have fun learning the relationship between letters, or groups of letters, and the sounds they represent.

This is an important step towards independent reading – it will enable your child to tackle new words by sounding out and blending their separate parts.